The Adventures of
David and Goliath

Goliath's
Birthday

Terrance Dicks
Illustrated by Valerie Littlewood

Piccadilly Press · London

Phototypeset by York House Typographic Ltd., London W7
Printed and bound by Biddles Ltd., Guildford and King's Lynn
for the publishers Piccadilly Press Ltd.,
5 Castle Road, London NW1 8PR

British Library Cataloguing in Publication Data
Dicks, Terrance
Goliath's Birthday (Adventures of David and Goliath: 12)
I. Title   II. Littlewood, Valerie   III. Series
893'.914 [J]   PZ7
ISBN 1-85340-075-0

Other titles in the series currently in print
GOLIATH'S EASTER PARADE
GOLIATH AT THE SEASIDE
GOLIATH GOES TO SUMMER SCHOOL
SPORTS DAY
GOLIATH AND THE CUB SCOUTS

Terrance Dicks lives in North London with his wife and three sons.
He is the author of over a hundred books for children, including
the *Dr Who* novelisations. Piccadilly Press publish several of his
series: *T.R. Bear, The Adventures of Buster & Betsy, Sally Ann,
Jonathan's Ghost,* and *A Cat Called Max.*

Valerie Littlewood lives in Lincolnshire with her husband, a dog
and a horse. As well as being a freelance illustrator, she is also an
art lecturer.

Chapter One

Be good, Goliath!

It all started one peaceful Sunday afternoon. Mum was reading a book, Dad was dozing over the paper, and Goliath was dozing on the hearthrug. David was passing the time by going through some old notebooks and diaries he'd found in a box in his room.

'Guess what?' said David suddenly. 'Next Saturday is Goliath's birthday!'

Goliath thumped his tail at the sound of his name.

'Are you sure?' asked Mum.

'Positive! I've just looked it up. We got him exactly five years ago next Saturday.'

'It certainly doesn't seem like five years ago does it?'

Dad looked up from his paper. 'More like fifty-five! When I think of what a happy peaceful life I had before that horrible hairy hound turned up . . . '

David's father wasn't too keen on Goliath just at the moment. Just recently there had been one or two little problems. Like the business with Marmalade and Mr MacGregor's garden.

Marmalade was a big ginger tomcat who belonged to Miss Marley two doors down. A few days ago, he had crept into the garden, sneaked up behind Goliath and taken a savage swipe at the

big dog's waving tail. Goliath had
yelped in alarm, turned round and
started chasing Marmalade.

Unfortunately Marmalade had shot
over the fence into Mr MacGregor's
garden. Goliath had bounded over the
fence after him, and the rest of the
chase had taken place round and
round Mr MacGregor's garden, most of
it over his beloved flower beds. And
Goliath was a big, heavy dog . . .

Mr MacGregor had come out to see what was happening and found his precious flower beds pretty well flattened. He'd turned the garden hose on them both, driving Marmalade on into his own garden, and Goliath back into his.

As soon as David's father got home from work an angry Mr MacGregor was banging on the door. It took quite a long while to soothe him down.

No sooner was that fuss over than Miss Marley turned up, and set about David's father for letting his horrible great dog chase her poor little pussy cat. No use telling her Marmalade had started it . . .

And as if all that hadn't been bad enough, next day there was the business with their landlady. Mrs Richards occupied the upper part of the house, and usually she and Goliath got on very well. But Goliath could be over-enthusiastic with people he was fond of, and he'd jumped up at Mrs Richards when she was coming home. Unfortunately, she'd been carrying a parcel – some antique glasses she'd just bought. David's dad had felt obliged to insist on paying for them, and they hadn't been cheap.

'We don't know when Goliath's actual birthday is,' said David's mum. 'I don't suppose anyone does now, not even the pet shop.'

David thought back to the day when they'd gone to buy a dog and he'd chosen the smallest puppy in the shop.

Even the pet shop lady had advised them not to buy him.

'You don't want him, he's the runt, smallest and weakest of the litter.

Sometimes they don't live very long . . . '

David had decided then and there that this was the puppy for him. He'd taken the miserable little creature home and named him Goliath, after the giant in the Bible.

He'd fed him and exercised him and loved and cared for him until Goliath had grown up strong and healthy.

More than that, Goliath, as if determined to live up to his name, had turned into the biggest dog for miles around.

David threw himself down beside Goliath and gave him a hug. 'We may not know his real birthday, but as far as I'm concerned, his birthday is the day we brought him back from the pet shop – and on Saturday next Goliath will be five years old!'

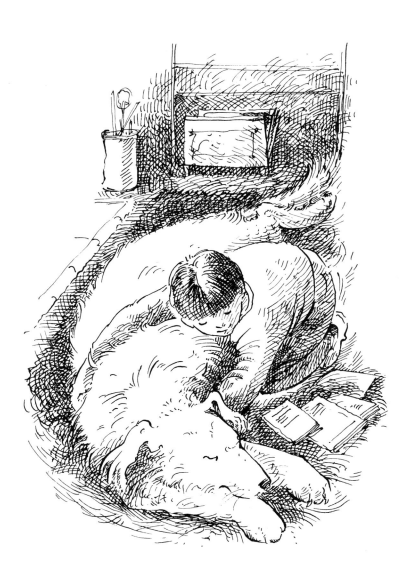

'That can be his Official Birthday,' said Mum. 'The Queen has an Official Birthday as well as her real one, so I don't see why Goliath can't have one too.'

'Good idea!' said David. 'We can have a party for him – Goliath's Official Birthday Party! We'll invite all his friends – Miss Hollings and Scrap, Mr Mountjoy and Mactavish, Nipper from down the launderette . . .'

'Oh no we won't,' said Dad. 'After all that animal's cost me in time, money and aggravation, I don't see that five years of Goliath is anything to celebrate!'

'Dad, *please* . . . ' said David.

'That's a bit hard, dear,' said David's mum.

'I know Goliath's been a bit unlucky recently,' said David, 'but he's a good

dog really – aren't you, Goliath?'

It took quite a bit more pleading, but eventually David's father gave in – well, almost. 'All right, I'll make a bargain with you. You reckon Goliath's birthday's next Saturday. If I don't get one single complaint about him from now till then – Goliath can have his birthday party!'

'No problem,' said David confidently.

9

'Goliath's going to be a *good dog* right up until his birthday! Aren't you, Goliath?'

Goliath wagged his tail and barked.

'See?' said David. 'He understands every word I say!'

Surprisingly enough, David was quite right.

That's what caused all the trouble . . .

Chapter Two

Goliath's Good Deeds

All through the next week, Goliath was good as gold.

David had taken quite a few precautions. He got his mother to promise to keep an eye on Goliath, and to shoo Marmalade away if he showed up in the garden.

He came home from school every lunch time and played with Goliath. Every evening he took Goliath for an extra long walk. His basic plan was to keep Goliath too busy, and too tired, to get into trouble.

The plan worked too – right up until the very last day.

It was Saturday morning, the day of Goliath's birthday. 'Well, we made it, Dad,' said David proudly. The invitations had been sent out and everyone had accepted.

'So you did,' agreed his father. 'Fancy old Goliath being thirty-five!'

David looked puzzled. 'He's five, not thirty-five.'

'Ah, but you have to reckon seven human years for every dog year,' said Mum. 'Your Dad's right, Goliath is a grown-up!'

'Him!' said Dad. 'He's as daft as the day we brought him home from the shop – dafter if anything!'

'No he isn't,' said David. 'Anyway,

you've got to admit, he's really been good this week. You're a good, grown-up dog – aren't you, Goliath?'

David and Goliath set off for the high street to shop for the party; cakes and biscuits for the humans, dog biscuits and dog treats for the dog guests. They were just passing the newsagents when they saw Mactavish coming out, followed by Mr Mountjoy, the old gentleman who was his master.

Mactavish was a black Scottie. He wore a little tartan coat of which he was very proud. Every day Mactavish's owner walked down to the paper shop to collect his morning paper. Every day he gave the rolled up newspaper to Mactavish who carried it home for him. As Mactavish came out of the shop, carrying the newspaper and looking very important, a passing old lady turned to her friend. 'Look, he's carrying the paper for his master! Isn't he a *good dog*!'

Goliath cocked his head and pricked up his ears. By now they were coming up to the butchers. Another old lady was just coming out, staggering under the weight of a heavy shopping bag. She put it down for a moment to rest – and Goliath seized his chance. He made a sudden dash, pulling his lead from David's hand. Picking up the shopping bag by the handles he trotted off.

For a moment the old lady was too astonished to speak.

Then she gave an ear-piercing yell. 'Stop him! Stop that dog! He's stolen my lamb chops!'

Goliath trotted on, feeling very pleased with himself. He heard the shouting and looked around. Dashing

after him was the owner of the chops, a tough, lively old lady who was still very nippy on her feet. 'It's a disgrace! Hairy great monsters snatching a poor old pensioner's dinner.'

Goliath was starting to feel worried. He couldn't quite make out what the old lady was saying, but it didn't sound much like, 'Oh what a good dog!'

The old lady dashed up and shouted, 'Take that!'

She made a savage swipe at him with her umbrella. 'Monster!' With a yelp of alarm, Goliath disappeared around the nearest corner, still carrying the bag . . .

David shot round the corner after him and grabbed the end of his trailing lead. 'Goliath, what do you think you're doing? You're supposed to be being good!'

He dragged Goliath back round the corner and up to the old lady, who was far from pleased. 'Is that your dog? He tried to steal my chops!'

'He didn't, honestly,' said David. If the old lady complained to his father . . . Already he could see the birthday party disappearing.

'Then why did he run off with my shopping bag?'

Suddenly David realised. 'He was trying to help! You see we saw this dog we know carrying his master's newspaper. Goliath just wanted to carry your bag for you.'

'Well, I never did,' said the old lady. David insisted on carrying her shopping home for her, and they parted good friends. She tried to give him 10p but David wouldn't take it. 'I'm a Cub Scout and this can be my good deed for the day!'

As they headed back to the high street David gave a sigh of relief. 'Well, that was a near one. I know you meant well, Goliath, but you can only carry things if people ask you to!'

Suddenly they saw a dog they knew coming up the street, a labrador called Sammy. There was a sort of leather harness on Sammy's body, and holding

on to reins fixed to the harness was a tall white-haired lady in dark glasses.

Goliath gave Sammy a friendly 'Woof!' and Sammy waved his tail in reply. The tall lady said, 'It's Goliath, isn't it, and David?'

'That's right,' said David. 'Good morning, Miss Markham.'

Sammy led her towards them, and she put out a hand and stroked Goliath's head. 'Can't stop, Goliath, we're going shopping. We'll see you at the party tonight. Come on, Sammy!'

Sammy led her to the zebra crossing and waited till the traffic stopped. Then he led her across the road and into the supermarket.

'It's wonderful the way she gets about,' said David. 'She does all her own shopping, you know. Sammy takes her everywhere. Miss Markham swears he knows all the different sections in the supermarket. Now there's a good dog for you, Goliath. Why can't you be more like Sammy?'

After buying the dog food they reached the bakers and David fixed Goliath's lead to the dog hook outside. 'I'm just going to get the cakes and

biscuits – you stay here, and don't get into any more trouble.'

Goliath sat down obediently on the pavement sniffing the appetising smells from the bakers. He was still thinking about what David had said. *'So, Sammy's a really good dog – now I know how to do it!'*

Goliath looked up and down the busy high street for someone to help. Suddenly he wagged his tail and barked excitedly. There coming towards him was a tall, skinny young man – and he was exactly the sort of person Goliath was looking for . . .

Chapter Three

Goliath the Guide Dog

Elvis Wilkins prided himself on being a colourful dresser. Today was his day off, and he was parading up and down the high street giving everyone a treat.

He was wearing ragged jeans, so ripped there was more rip than jeans, half-laced baseball boots, a T-shirt with a smiling face on, a brightly-coloured yellow windcheater and a baseball cap, worn backwards.

But the finishing touch, the thing

Elvis was really proud of, was the glasses, small round ones with thick black lenses.

To Elvis, his dark glasses added the final touch of trendiness.

To Goliath they were the sign he was looking for.

In his eagerness to help, Goliath strained at his lead – and the dog hook, which was old and rusty, pulled right out of the wall. Goliath bounded up to Elvis and gave him an encouraging 'Woof!', just to show he was all ready to help.

Nervously, Elvis backed away. He was a bit scared of dogs, and Goliath was the biggest dog he'd ever seen.

Goliath woofed again and cocked his head, wondering what was the matter. *'I'm wearing my lead, why doesn't the human hold on so I can take him across the road? If he won't hold on to me, I'll just have to hold on to him!'*

Goliath grabbed Elvis by the leg of his tattered jeans and started dragging him towards the zebra crossing.

'Leggo!' yelled Elvis, pulling away – and the ragged edge of his jeans came away in Goliath's teeth.

Dropping the chunk of material, Goliath grabbed the other leg.

Elvis tried to hop away.'Leggo!' he yelled. 'Gerroff!'

The second leg ripped . . .

By now Goliath was getting impatient. *'I'm trying to help this human and all he does is yell at me!'* he thought, dropping the second bit of trouser-leg.

As Elvis turned to run, Goliath grabbed him by the seat of his jeans and heaved him towards the zebra crossing.

Elvis struggled wildly – and the whole of the middle bit of the jeans tore away.

Elvis's belt was now supporting just a ragged fringe of denim. Below his knees were the remnants of his trouser-legs, like tattered leg-warmers. In between there was nothing but his Union Jack boxer shorts.

As the rest of the jeans tore away, Elvis pulled himself free. Too panic-stricken to realise what he was doing, he dashed across the zebra crossing and into the supermarket.

The crowd of shoppers greeted the trouserless Elvis's sudden appearance with shrieks of horror. 'Pervert!' yelled one of them, whacking him over the head with her shopping basket.

'It's one of those streaker fellas!' shouted an angry retired colonel, flourishing his umbrella. 'Disgraceful!'

A mob of angry shoppers chased Elvis out of the supermarket and up the steps of the police station . . .

On the other side of the road, Goliath stood watching in amazement. *'Well, at least I tried!'* he thought.

The bakers had been crowded and busy and David came out with his bag of cakes and biscuits quite unaware of what had been going on.

He found Goliath standing on the

pavement looking puzzled, with the rusty iron hook on the pavement nearby. 'Now what have you been doing? Honestly, you just don't know your own strength!' Sticking the hook back into the hole in the wall, David led Goliath back home.

His parents were out visiting David's grandmother, so David and Goliath were alone in the house. David made a cup of tea, awarded Goliath and himself just one party cake in advance, and settled down for some Saturday morning telly. Goliath stared eagerly at the screen hoping to see some cartoons.

But instead of Bugs Bunny or Tom and Jerry, the screen showed a big green field with a scattering of humans and animals.

There was a sort of open pen in the middle of the field and there was a

group of white woolly things huddled by the gate.

One of the dogs was driving the woolly things towards the pen. He did this by making little dashes to get them moving, then lying down to see which way they went. If they tried to move in the wrong direction, the dog would circle round and make another dash to get them back on course again. Gradually he got the whole wandering group safely inside the pen.

'They're really clever, those sheep-dogs,' said David. 'Look at the way he got those sheep in the pen. There's another good dog for you, Goliath . . . '

Chapter Four

Disaster on the Farm

Goliath pricked up his ears. *'A good dog! Just for chasing a few of those woolly things about. I could do that easily!'*

The trouble was, where would he find them?

Suddenly Goliath remembered something. He jumped up and started barking.

David looked at him in amazement. 'Now what?'

Goliath ran to the door and barked

again.

'You want to go out?' asked David. 'We've only just got in – and anyway, it's just started to rain!'

Goliath barked yet again and David said, 'All right, all right, we'll go for a walk.' David swigged his tea, put on his coat, put Goliath on his lead and they set off.

When they reached the edge of the common, David took Goliath off the lead. Usually Goliath dashed round in circles barking, but this time he just shot off in a straight line. 'Now what's got into him?' thought David. 'He seems to be heading for the adventure playground.'

The adventure playground was a ramshackle collection of rope swings and climbing frames, concrete tunnels, wooden platforms and brightly painted petrol drums. There was a big hut attached to the playground, and a group of cheerful young volunteers to arrange activities.

David set off after Goliath, who was already disappearing into the distance. 'What's he so keen to go there for?' thought David. 'Come to that, why was he so keen to come out? Usually he hates the rain. We were watching that programme about sheep-dogs and – oh no!' David broke into a run. The adventure playground had just added a new attraction. In a tiny field just behind the hut they'd set up what they called their urban farm.

It wasn't nearly as grand as the name suggested – just a sheep, a goat, some rabbits and guinea pigs and hens. They were nearly all animals you could stroke and feed and pet, and they gave town kids the chance to see some real farm animals . . .

Goliath remembered visiting the place with David when it first opened. *'I'm sure there's at least one of the woolly things for me to herd,'* he thought as he loped towards it.

Because of the drizzling rain, the adventure playground was deserted when Goliath arrived. But there was plenty going on inside. The big hut was filled with children, busily painting and drawing and modelling with lovely messy clay.

The urban farm was deserted too. The sheep and the goat were grazing peacefully in different corners of the field, the rabbits and guinea pigs munching happily away in their pens, and the hens clucking around their henhouse in a separate enclosure.

'*Time to do a bit of herding!*' thought Goliath.

He jumped over the fence, dashed up to the sheep and threw himself down, like the dog on the television.

The sheep looked up, stared at Goliath in amazement, and went on grazing. Goliath dashed a bit closer,

threw himself down again and gave a tremendous 'Woof!' to encourage it.

The sheep replied with an indignant 'Baa!' and trotted away.

'That's more like it!' thought Goliath.

He made another dash, and the sheep moved a bit further away. Not really bothered, it lowered its head and started eating again.

'This herding is dead easy', thought Goliath.

But he'd reckoned without the goat. It was a big, black billy goat called Satan because of its evil nature and terrible temper. It didn't much like dogs at the best of times, and it certainly didn't like dogs chasing its friends the sheep. Lowering its head it gave a fierce bray, a sort of 'Behh!' and charged towards Goliath with such force it snapped its tether.

Goliath heard the strange sound, turned and saw a huge black monster tearing towards him. Its slanting eyes were blazing and it had big fierce-looking horns.

Deciding it wasn't the sort of thing you could herd, Goliath made a run for it. He jumped up, tore across the field and jumped over the fence into the adventure playground, Satan close behind him. The goat chased Goliath right round the adventure playground, through the tunnels and over the jumps. It was a tough, sure-footed animal and it was gaining fast.

Deciding he needed some human help with this dangerous monster, Goliath dashed for the hut.

The art teacher, a large commanding sort of woman, was just saying, 'Now remember children, a smooth clay mix is absolutely essential,' when Goliath swept into the hut like a huge hairy tornado. The children in the class jumped up and yelled excitedly, and there was instant uproar.

But Goliath's entrance was nothing compared to Satan's.

Tearing into the hut, the goat jumped up on to one of the work tables and ran along it sending pots of paint and bowls of clay flying in all directions.

Jumping off the table, the goat looked round for Goliath. Instead it saw the art mistress bending over with her back to him to pick up a fallen bowl. Unable to resist such a tempting target, Satan lowered his head and charged . . .

The art mistress flew through the air and landed on another table which

collapsed beneath her weight.

Two of the bigger children grabbed the goat by the collar. While they were struggling with it, Goliath, who had been cowering in a corner, shot through the door and ran straight into David who had been chasing madly after him.

David took one horrified look at the scene of wreckage inside the hut. It was full of overturned easels and tables and excited helpers and yelling children. Everything and everyone seemed to be covered in paint and clay. David knew he ought to go in and explain but he just didn't dare. Grabbing Goliath by the collar he heaved him away.

It was later that afternoon, and David and Goliath were back at home. Goliath was watching television – cartoons at last – and David was wondering what to do next. He knew the playground helpers quite well and had once helped them with a fund-raising carnival. Perhaps he could explain and persuade them not to complain to his dad. If not, Goliath's birthday party was doomed . . .

The doorbell rang and David went to answer it. A tall young man with reddish brown hair and a beaky nose was standing on the doorstep. 'Hello, David,' he said. 'Remember me? Constable Foskett. I gave a talk to your Cub Pack not long ago.'

'Sorry, didn't recognise you out of uniform. What can I do for you?'

'Well, do you think I could pop in for a quick word?'

David remembered his parents' warning about letting people in the house, but he supposed the police were different, and he did know Constable Foskett. 'Yes, of course, come on in.'

He led Constable Foskett into the living room, where Goliath was absorbed in a Tom and Jerry cartoon.

Constable Foskett looked hard at Goliath and said, 'Yes, that's the dog all right, no doubt about it.' He put a hand on Goliath's collar and said solemnly, 'Goliath, you're under arrest!'

Chapter Five

Tally Ho!

David looked at the young policeman in amazement. 'You're not serious? What's Goliath supposed to have been up to?'

'Assault and battery, incitement to riot, wanton destruction of property including livestock.'

'Oh, no,' said David guiltily, 'I didn't realise things were that bad.'

'Well,' said Constable Foskett, 'it's like this. I called in the high street police station today and they seem to have been having a doggie crime wave. First of all some young man dashes in, wearing boxer shorts and dark glasses, chased by a mob of angry shoppers. *They* say he's a streaker, *he* says a big shaggy dog attacked him and stole his trousers.'

David stared at him. 'We were in the high street this morning – and Goliath got loose while I was in the bakers – but why would he steal anyone's trousers? Hang on a minute – did you say the man was wearing dark glasses?'

'Apparently. Why, is it important?'

'I'm afraid this is all my fault,' said David. 'We'd just been talking to Miss Markham, you see, and I remember praising her guide dog. Goliath must have been trying to be a guide dog, like Sammy. Because that poor chap was wearing dark glasses he tried to help him across the road – and ended up stealing his trousers!'

'I'm afraid there's more,' said Constable Foskett. 'Later on, they got an angry phone call from the adventure playground. Apparently some big hairy dog attacked their livestock, broke up an art class and wrecked their recreation hut.'

David sighed. 'He was only trying to be a sheep-dog like the ones on television. That was my fault as well.'

'When all the fuss was over, they found one of their chickens dead in the henhouse – and another one had disappeared.'

'Now that *wasn't* Goliath,' said David definitely.

'Anyway,' said Constable Foskett, 'I remembered meeting a certain big shaggy dog when I was talking to the Cubs, so I phoned Akela, got your address and popped round for a chat.'

'What happens now?'

'They decided the man with no trousers had suffered enough so they didn't charge him. They lent him a blanket to cover his confusion and gave him a cup of tea and a ride home in a police car. With luck you might not hear any more about that. But the chickens could mean real trouble. The lady who runs the art class owns the chickens and she's really steamed up.'

'I told you, Goliath didn't do that!'

'I just hope you can convince the playground people.' Constable Foskett stood up. 'I didn't really come round to arrest Goliath you know, more to give you a friendly warning, and a chance to sort things out.'

When Constable Foskett had gone, David turned to Goliath. 'We'd better go to the adventure playground and try to explain . . . '

It was dusk by the time they reached the adventure playground and David went cautiously up to the door of the hut. It was all neat and clean again inside, and a helper called Mike and a gang of kids were doing the last of the cleaning up.

Mike looked up as David and Goliath appeared. 'I was wondering when you

two would turn up.'

'I've got a confession to make,' said David.

Mike grinned. 'It's all right, we know it was Goliath, lots of us recognised him.'

'I'm sorry about his wrecking the class.'

'That's all right, I think the kids enjoyed it – and Satan the goat certainly did. I'd say forget it – if it wasn't for the chicken business . . . '

'But that wasn't Goliath! I was right behind him. He went straight into the farm, then the goat chased him in here. He didn't go near the chickens.'

'I believe you,' said Mike, 'but I doubt if Miss Carter the art teacher will. She'll say you're just trying to protect Goliath.'

David was thinking hard. 'Well,

somebody or something took those chickens. Can I take a look at the scene of the crime?'

Everything was deserted as they walked over to the little enclosure. The sheep and the big black goat were grazing peacefully. There was no sign of the chickens, no doubt they were all roosting in the henhouse.

David examined the muddy ground around the little hut. Goliath ran

around, sniffing eagerly. Suddenly he barked, and David went over to him. 'What's up, Goliath?'

Goliath looked down and whined. In the fading light, David could just see tracks, oddly-shaped footprints, leading towards the adventure playground.

'Those aren't your tracks,' said David. 'Seek, Goliath, seek!' Led by Goliath, they followed the tracks across the playground to a rusting oil drum, abandoned on its side in the far corner. Goliath was sniffing hard now, and as they reached the drum he began barking excitedly. Suddenly a long, low, reddish shape streaked out of the drum with something white in its mouth.

'It's a fox!' yelled Mike. 'After him. Tally ho!'

Goliath had had enough of strange creatures. He could still remember the goat. He stood there wagging his tail and barking as the fox disappeared into the dusk, never to be seen again.

'It's an urban fox,' said David. 'I saw

a programme about them on the television. Mostly they just live on rubbish and scraps. This one must have been pleased to find some nice fat chickens.'

'An urban fox for an urban farm,' said Mike. 'I'll get on to Miss Carter straight away and explain. She'll have to put a good strong wire fence round that chicken run.'

'Come on, Goliath,' said David, 'we'd better get home. We've got a party to prepare for.' He turned to Mike. 'Tell you what, why don't you and the kids come as well? It's Goliath's Official Birthday!'

Goliath's Official Birthday Party was a great success. Goliath got a new collar and lead, a brush, a comb and a blanket and, just for once, all the cakes and doughnuts he could eat.

'Well, you made it,' said David's father, looking round the living room, now bulging with grown-ups, dogs and kids. 'A whole week, and not a single complaint about Goliath!'

David grinned. 'We had one or two narrow shaves though, Dad.' He gave Goliath a big hug. 'Considering all the trouble you caused trying to be grown-up and good, I think you'd better stay your old silly self!'